Sawdust Carpets

STORY AND PICTURES BY

Amelia Lau Carling

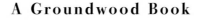

A Groundwood Book

Douglas & McIntyre   Toronto   Vancouver   Berkeley

For my family

Groundwood Books / Douglas & McIntyre
720 Bathurst Street, Suite 500, Toronto, Ontario M5S 2R4
Distributed in the USA by Publishers Group West
1700 Fourth Street, Berkeley, CA 94710

Library and Archives Canada Cataloguing in Publication
Carling, Amelia Lau
Sawdust Carpets / story and pictures by Amelia Lau Carling.
ISBN 0-88899-625-X
I. Title.
PZ7.C2165Sa 2005   j813'.54   C2004-905054-0

The illustrations were done in watercolor, pastels and colored pencil.
Printed and bound in China

Prologue

The week before Easter is called Holy Week. In Antigua, Guatemala, originally a colonial city built by the Spaniards in the late 1500s, processions of people carrying centuries-old statues wind through the streets, re-enacting the story of Christ's death and resurrection. This tradition is as strong as it was when the Spaniards introduced it long ago, though it has been transformed by its contact with Guatemalan native culture.

As offerings of their faith, neighbors create carpets out of colored sawdust, flowers and fruit that lie directly in the path of the processions. Year after year they make rugs with new designs. Year after year the processions walk over them, destroying their elaborate patterns as they move on.

When I was growing up in Guatemala, my family's household was a Chinese one that kept to its own customs. But Holy Week was like no other week, even for a Chinese family as traditional as ours. With neighbors we gathered on the sidewalks to see the carpets before the corteges marched over them. As we watched the processions, I felt as if the story they told was happening right then. And the beauty of the short-lived tapestries, so lovingly made, has stayed in my heart.

The color of Holy Week is purple. That's why Mami sold so many yards of violet cloth during the Easter season. One day the mailman delivered an envelope with silver letters written on it.

"Una invitación!" cried Mami. She couldn't read Spanish very well, so my sister took it.

"It says that Tío Colocho and Tía Malía invite us to the baby's baptism on Easter Sunday."

A piece of paper written in Chinese fell out of the envelope. Mami read it because although we understood when spoken to, we couldn't read anything in Chinese. "We are also asked to their house to spend Holy Week before the baptism… Let's go!" cried Mami happily. We jumped for joy.

On Maundy Thursday we piled into our rusty car and drove to the old city of Antigua. Papa filled the trunk with our things, adding a box of soft drinks and a basket of oranges. On the way we sang like mariachis on the radio. *Ay ayay ay…*

We knew we were in Antigua when the car rumbled over the cobbled streets. *Bum, bum, bulum.*

Tío Colocho, Tía Malía and our cousins were waiting at the door of their store. To fit us all in, they had set up a table in the middle of the shop where we ate supper.

Cantonese words flew through the air. We told jokes with our cousins and laughed and laughed. Something in the corner of the room caught my eye.

There stood the Virgin of Guadalupe next to the Kuan Yin, our Chinese goddess. I thought they looked like friends. Incense swirled around them, bringing them together.

Mami said to Tía Malía in Chinese, "Remember when we were children in China? We went to the bridge to see the boats race down the river."

Tía Malía smiled. "It was the Dragon Boat Festival. On that day we would throw Chinese tamales into the river, for good luck." They laughed and then grew quiet, maybe thinking of those long-gone days.

Tía Malía said, "Niños, tomorrow at dawn there will be a procession from La Merced, the church at the end of the street. The neighbors are making sawdust carpets all along the block. Go and see."

Sawdust carpets!

On the sidewalk I saw nets brimming with pine needles, purple and yellow blossoms and sunflowers. There were sacks full of sawdust dyed in brilliant colors — magenta, turquoise, orange and green. Pods of corozo flowers filled the air with the sweet smell of sea and palm trees.

Don Ortiz, who lived across the street, was making a rug. First he laid out a layer of natural sawdust and wet it. Then his helpers drew on it with colored sawdust. They climbed on boards to reach the places that they had to decorate without disturbing what was already done. With sifters they showered colors through cardboard stencils. They measured the designs carefully following don Ortiz's instructions. Then a helper went over the whole rug with a fine sprinkling of water — *pish, pish* — so that the sawdust would stay flat.

Ay, how beautiful it was. It looked like a real carpet!

"Do you want to help, niña?" asked don Ortiz when he noticed me staring.

I jumped up and cried, "Sí, señor, don Ortiz!"

"Bring over that red sawdust for the roses and the flour for the white lilies. And find the smallest sifter because these flowers are very delicate." Over the tapestry of colored sawdust the artisans laid sunflowers, corozo blossoms and pine needles.

One by one carpets appeared down the street. It was getting dark and Tía Malía said, "Go to bed. The procession will go by early in the morning."

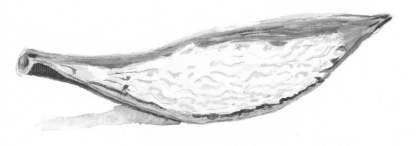

Good Friday was foggy at dawn. There were a lot of people waiting outside the church. Don Ortiz, dressed as a cucurucho, saw us and said, "Kids, do you want the leftover sawdust?"

"Sí, señor," I answered excitedly. "Everyone, let's make a little rug. Let's make a house. Hurry, the procession is coming!"

We quickly made a hut with a red roof and yellow walls. We used purple sawdust for the sky and pine needles for grass. We laid down branches of bugambilia.

Petals from the flowers in the patio were just right for a heart. We added stars and comets to the sky using fistfuls of rice and sunflowers. I just managed to lay out a border of oranges and give our carpet a final sprinkle of water. Qué lindo!

Someone whispered, "The procession is starting!"

At the thunder of a great big drum, *pon... pon... pon,* the cucuruchos lifted a huge wooden platform onto their shoulders. On it a statue of Jesus carried the Cross. He was surrounded by orchids and mosses from the forest. His eyes shone and my heart beat *pon... pon.* His crown of thorns and the blood on his face made me quiver. The people outside the church fell on their knees.

The Christ swayed to the sad music played by the band that marched behind the procession. He seemed like a real person.

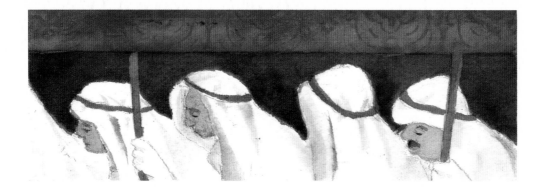

The purple cucuruchos bent under the weight on their shoulders as white incense swirled around them.

The Virgin Mary followed, carried by women. A sword thrust into her heart showed her great pain. She cried crystal tears because her Son was going to die soon. The band behind her played a march to console her and us, too.

The procession had reached our part of the street.

Suddenly I realized that the cucuruchos were really going to walk on our beautiful rug! With each step, my heart tightened. I stood in front of our carpet. I did not want them to destroy it. "Don't pass here. Don't pass," I was thinking.

Don Ortiz took me by the hand and pulled. "Niñita! This is the custom. We make the rugs as offerings to life. Haven't you noticed? Flowers bloom and soon they die, but they leave seeds so others will grow. Life follows death and death follows life."

I couldn't stop them. *Pon… pon… pon…* Step by step the feet of the cucuruchos tore the grass, the walls and the roof of our house. They erased the stars and the comets. They smeared the colors. They trampled the flowers and kicked the oranges here and there.

Our rug was a sad river that ran down the middle of the street, smelling of sea and palm trees.

We followed the band. In the afternoon, under the blazing sun, the procession of the Holy Sepulcher traveled slowly through the cobbled streets. By now Christ had died. There were men dressed as Romans and the cucuruchos, now dressed in black, carried the dead Christ in a splendid golden and crystal coffin.

We wandered through the lanes looking for other processions. Mostly, we found the ruins of beautiful carpets.

That night we walked home feeling tired and sad.

The next day, on Saturday, Mami and Tía Malía cooked Chinese tamales for the baptism party.

"The processions are so moving," they said in Chinese.

Mami added, "They're beautiful like the festivals of our home in China. They come and go every year, and each time they're different."

On Easter Sunday the church was dressed in happy colors because it was the day of the resurrection, when Christ came back to life.

My little cousin was baptized. They named him Angel. Angel Sen Quan. When they poured water – *pish* – over his head, his cry echoed under the cupola.

That afternoon, at the party, don Ortiz talked about the carpet he would make next year. He planned one with doves and loaves of bread in the form of crocodiles. I began to think how I would make another one, too, this time with butterflies and birds.

Don Ortiz was right. We made the rug for the procession. When it was destroyed, we could think about making another one.

In the corner, the Virgin of Guadalupe and the Kuan Yin glowed in the warmth of the candle.

We had a big piñata on the patio. It was my turn to give it the last blow.

I broke the clay jar that was inside it and *pum*! It landed on my head. The candy leaped all over. My little cousin, Angel, thought it was very funny!

And that's how Holy Week ended.

Glossary

bugambilia

corozo

Virgin of Guadalupe

cucurucho

Kuan Yin

tamales

bugambilia Bougainvillea, a tropical vine with bright-colored blossoms that grows easily over walls and roofs.

corozo The aromatic cream-colored blossoms that grow inside the large pod of a palm tree. These blossoms are used as decoration during Eastertime.

cucurucho (coo-coo-roo-cho) In Guatemala, a man or boy who dresses in a traditional purple gown and participates in the processions during Holy Week.

don The respectful form of address for "Sir."

Dragon Boat Festival A Chinese festival remembering an official who dared speak against a cruel emperor. Crowds gather to watch boat races and throw dumplings into the water to feed his spirit.

Good Friday A deeply religious day when the most solemn and dramatic processions take place in Antigua, Guatemala. Three o'clock in the afternoon symbolizes the time of Christ's death. At this time cucuruchos, dressed in black instead of purple, carry the Christ in his coffin, the Holy Sepulcher. Processions travel the streets from dawn to midnight.

Kuan Yin The Chinese Buddhist goddess of mercy.

mariachis Mexican folk musicians.

Maundy Thursday The Thursday before Easter Sunday. A day of meditation and preparation for Good Friday.

niña, niñita Girl, little girl.

niños Children.

piñata A gaily decorated creature made out of paper and filled with candy.

qué lindo How pretty.

señor The respectful form of address for "Mr."

tamale In Guatemala, a corn dumpling wrapped in banana leaves. In China, a rice dumpling wrapped in bamboo or lotus leaves.

tío, tía Uncle, aunt.

Virgin of Guadalupe The Virgin Mary who appeared miraculously in Mexico. She is venerated throughout Latin America.